ATTENTION: SCHOOLS AND BUSINESSES

My Home My Body can and should be bought in bulk while supplies last.

for all those who have been abused

such as myself

this year has seen much progress in

the end of this monstrous act

we have fought and won

many battles that have left us forever

scarred

but still

we have many wars left to go

before our wounded souls can

finally rest

- *the war has just begun my sisters*

contents

life

i walk around

carrying luggage

thinking one day

i will find

a home

- shelter

like a tree

my roots

run deep

and no matter how

hard you push

i shall hold

my ground

-life

like a rubber ball

you think i'll

keep bouncing back

to

you

they told her

she needed to find

a knight

when all she needed

was to

find a sword

i have walked into

cemeteries looking

for my headstone

but no

i did not die the day

you

tore apart my heart

-still alive

he won't be coming back

waiting for someone

who has found another

wastes minutes of your life

you can't get back

he will realize one day

his greatest loss was

your biggest gain

- too late / too little

###

#MeToo

a man can tell a 1,000 lies

and its

uncontested as the truth

a woman can tell 1 truth

and its

contested like she told a 1,000 lies

- *#MeToo*

at my apartment that night

i filled the tub with scalding hot water

tossed in dill from the backyard garden

four teaspoons of peanut oil

half cup of sweetened coconut milk

one tablespoon of raw honey

a dash of salt

a pinch of turmeric

rose petals i stole from the mexican florist on the corner

i soaked myself in the stew

desperate to wash the filth off

the first hour

i picked cockleburs from my hair

counted them one two three five seven forty twenty two six

lined them up on edge of the tub

the second hour

i sobbed like a fat boy denied a third helping of supper

a howling escaped me

who knew girl could become wolf

on the third hour

i found bits of him embedded on bits of me

the perspiration was not mine

the creamy white between my legs

not mine

the stench of cheap cologne

not mine

the blood

mine

the fourth hour i prayed

it felt like you heaved me

so far from who I was

i've been trying to find my way back to myself ever since

- *find my way back*

sex requires consent between both

if one is lying there drunk or

passed out or simply not in the mood

yet the other is trying to slip his cock into her

ass

it is not love

it is rape

- *sodomy*

in cruel situations

remain kind

but carry a knife and

mace

because men will try to

force themselves into you like

they own whats beneath

your panties

as if you only exist

as a means for their sexual appetites

drive the blade into their hearts

my sisters

and blind them with truth

you are not here to be meat for wolves

you are here to be queens among overlords

the light in a world of patriarchal darkness

- without consent is worth killing for my sisters

i can't remember

because i can't recall

it was late

i passed out at some point in

his hotel room

he asked me to meet him there

to discuss a live poetry reading event

to be held at madison square garden

it was too good to be true

he told me to have a drink

i did because it was polite

he asked me to have another

i did because his tone became harsh

it got hot in the room

i took off my shirt to cool down

he asked if i brought my poetry

i did and pulled it out of my bag

i caught his lustful eyes groping at my breasts

i handed him the papers

it was unbearably hot so i took my pants off

i was sweating there in my underwear and bra

he said the poems sounded wonderful

something the world should hear

i smiled and felt like my big break had come

then i woke up

that morning

naked and feeling violated on that couch

he was cooking breakfast like

nothing happened the night before

but i know what i felt

it felt like he used his position to

take advantage of my dreams and passion

he knew he had power in this industry

and i was disposal to him like a single use razor

but i'm not

no no no

this is me cutting him as deep as he cut me

you will wear this scar like i bear yours

- #MeToo

february 24, 2020

on this day

justice was served

my sisters

how old men will say

our women must wear clothes that covers their entire face

just the eyes can be seen

only your husband can see your hair and

your plaid skirt must end at your ankles

keep your legs covered

keep your legs folded over each other until

your husband commands you to divide them

old men will say god whispered these instructions to them

and so they are merely passing them along to you

funny

but i doubt our mother in the heavens would be more

concerned with us being loving and kind souls

than if the guy handing me my pork sandwich can see my full face

if my coworker can see my beautiful hair

if my skirt is above my knee showing my toned legs

or if i choose to divide my legs for any man i desired

i think these old men saying they speak for god

actually speak for the devil

trying to shackle women in order to keep us

from rising above them

- fly my sisters

house

it began as a typical friday night from what i recall

sunlight kissed my lips good morning

i remember it exactly

climbing out of my tempur pedic bed

making coffee to the sound of fat children playing outside

putting reggaeton music on

despacito blaring as i

loaded my dirty clothes into the washer

i remember placing white roses in a vase

in the middle of the kitchen table

only when my apartment was as pure as those petals

did i step into the bathtub

wash last night out of my hair

i decorated myself

like the walls of any home are decorated

with frames bookshelves photos

i hung a necklace of pearls around my neck

hooked earrings in like a puerto rican chula

applied lipstick like paint

swept my hair back—just your typical friday

we ended up at a party with mutual friends

at the end you asked if i needed a ride back home and

i said *yes* cause our dads worked on the same goat farm

and you'd been to my place for dinner all the time

but i should have known

when you began to confuse

kind conversation with flirtation

when you told me to let my hair down and unbutton my top

when instead of driving me home

of lights and life—you took a left

to the road that led nowhere

i asked if you liked lana del rey and where we were going

you said no and asked if i was afraid

my voice flung itself over the edge of my throat

landed at the bottom of my bowels and hid there for months

all the different parts in me

like a switch you turned all the lights off in me

shut the blinds

locked the doors

while i hid at the back of some

upstairs room of my mind as

someone shattered the windows—you

straight kicked the front door in—you

took everything

and then somcone took me

—it was you.

who barreled into me with a fork and a knife

eyes glinting with starvation like a lion on the attack

like you hadn't eaten in years

i was a hundred and thirty eight pounds of fresh meat

you tore apart and disemboweled with your claws

like you were scraping the inside of a watermelon clean

licking the sweet tasty fruit juice from your nails

as i screamed for my mother

you hammered my wrists to the ground

turned my breasts into spoiled fruit

this house is empty now

no gas

no running water

no electricity

the food is expired

from head to toe i am covered in shit and piss

fruit flies. cockroaches. spiders. termites.

someone call the plumber

my colon is backed up—i haven't taken a shit since

call con ed

my eyes don't light up

when you broke into my house

it has never felt like mine again

i try to let new lovers in but i get sick

i lose sleep thinking of that first date

I cannot eat

become a skeleton with no skin

cannot remember how to breathe

every night my house becomes a psych ward

where panic attacks turns millennial beta men

into quasi retarded doctors to keep me calm

every lover who puts a finger on me—feels like you

their hands—you

lips—you

until they're not the ones

on top of me—it's you

and i am so exhausted

of doing things

—it isn't working

i've spent decades trying to figure it out

how i could have stopped it

but the moon can't stop the hurricane from coming

the oak can't stop the ax

i can't blame myself for having this hole

the size of texas in my chest anymore

your guilt is too heavy—i'm setting it down

i'm tired of wallpapering my walls with your shame

as if it is mine

i cannot walk around with it

what your cock did to me

what your hands have done

it wasn't my hands that did it

the truth comes to me suddenly—after years of clouds

the truth comes like sunlight peeking through the darkness

pouring in through the blinds of my windows

it took a long time to get here

but it came full circle like an apple pie

it takes a broken person to come looking

for meaning between my legs

it takes a complete. whole. perfectly constructed

person to survive it

it takes demons to steal souls

and angles to reclaim them

this house is the only house i came into this world with

was the first house

it is my only house

you can't take it

there is no room in it for you

no welcome mat on the floor

no extra closet space

i'm opening the living room windows

airing it out

putting white roses in a vase

in the middle of the kitchen table

lighting a blunt

cleaning my dirty socks and panties

until they're no stains on either

scrubbing the bathroom tiles like a mexican housekeeper

and then

i plan to step into my tub

wash last night out of my hair

rub my clit until i cum

finger my asshole a little

then put my feet up

and enjoy

this typical friday night

in a body that no longer feels like my own

because this place had been broken into

because you vandalized my—

- *house*

be careful with love

my father instructed

boys will dissolve that pill over your cup

when your back is turned

and when you wake up the next day

naked from the waist down

you will learn the hard way never to

take a drink from cupid's cup

- poison arrows / cups

how does it feel

to be the exploited

rather than the exploiter

crazy / beautiful

people are like

haunted houses

full

of ghosts

they tend to scare away

anyone looking to build

a home with them

- *haunted houses*

like a bee

in search of nectar

you landed on my petals

took what you needed

and then

flew away

stealing my sweetness

a thief left me stung

- the relationship between a bee and the flower

you were too busy

banging trash cans

when you could've

been banging me

on the first day of love

my heart mended inside my body

flowers wilting

the earth is tilting

still i wait for you

in the same spot

you left me

rupi!

my father screamed

why come you never shave your legs?!

you look like cousin it!

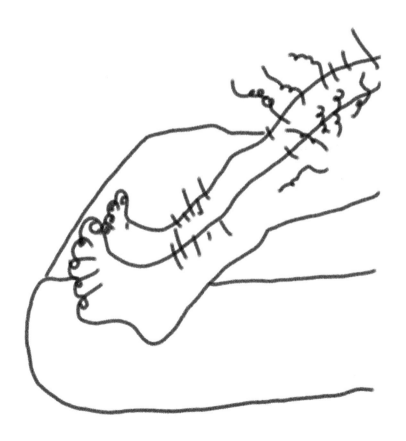

i once played softball

the coach

a lesbian named

henry

told me to tuck

my sack back

to this day

i still do

if you are

blowing a guy

and you fart

i think its okay to laugh

and for the guy to

laugh too

because

come on

life is funny

we used to laugh

at papa

when he would go off into town

with a coat made of goat skins

and sheep wool

we would not be laughing that evening

when he would come back

with some

whore he picked up

on the road back home

the crows seem to be

calling his name

thought caw

papa always said

laughter is the best medicine

which i guess is why

several of us

died of the flu

time is precious

and it is slipping away

and

i have been waiting

for you

all of my life

i wish you

could see how

i smile when

i read your morning

text messages

quaden

you've got a friend in me

- antibullying / stand with quaden

you have been told

since day one

you are a woman

but what if

on day two

you felt like a man

perhaps on wednesday you

feel like both

or maybe you feel like

neither

you identify as you wish

be whatever

be you

the man at the door said

sorry this bathroom is

only for men

I told him

so then why are you standing here

- gender neutral toilets

from the darkest

smelliest of places

if you plant

a warm

load of seeds

something will eventually

explode

out of it

take a deep sniff

like a cab

you picked me up

only to

drop me off elsewhere

hugh is a friend of

quaden too

- jackman is a true superhero

you broke in

through the front

when you used to

sneak in

through

my backdoor

if rehab means

losing you

consider

me a junkie

shooting you into

my veins

i'm a bed

you're a sheet

drape yourself

over me

spend my days

stuck in

a haze

trying to forget you

like the desserts miss

the rains

i am

not

your dog

do not

try to

curb me

stand with quaden

- bully the bullies

find someone who will

ruin your lipstick

not your

mascara

-*smear my lipstick*

i am a many faced

goddess

last night i hugged my chinese deliveryman

no virus will stop me from loving

it is god testing our compassion

your name is not

mcdonald

so why

do you ask me

to spread my buns

for your big mac

-*you want my fish filet*

our hearts

bleed stories

no surgeon

can stitch

shut

i've stood

on a forked

road

not knowing which

direction

to take

i am far away

from when i

started this

journey

tell me

if you still

love me

sun rays peeking

through

gray clouds

you were that

ray of light

in my endless

night

my heart

is bleeding

but I have

hungry eyes

i want to be

your prisoner

beat me with kisses

jail me with hugs

kill me with

love

white wedding dresses

flying doves

rice being tossed

curry chicken at my reception

limos waiting

love being made

goats being milked and honey being

squeezed into cups of warm goat's milk

- *my punjabi girl fantasies*

i wonder

how is it going

to be

when you are

not with me

anymore

it tears up

my heart

when im with you

but when we are

apart i feel it too

no matter what we do

i feel the same

baby

with or without you

i don't wanna close

my eyes

i don't wanna fall asleep

cause i will miss you babe

and I don't wanna miss a thing

tears on my pillow

there was a recipe of life

said my father

as he held me by the hand and i wept

think of these sheep as you tend to them

they will teach you

that people too

must be tended to daily

fed

given water

and led by a wise shepherd

or they risk breaking off and

losing their ways

i looked at him as one would

a wise man

and said

oh

- father was wise

i think

my heart knew

you would not stay

- *abandoned*

i longed

for you

but you wanted

someone else

i deny the one

who longed for me

cause i longed for someone else

- *the heart wants what it wants*

yesterday

the sun tried to imitate my feet

by covering your face in her rays

i ripped the heavens apart for allowing it

- god is a bitch named karma santiago rosalita lopez

the songbirds sing to me

you've changed your ways

i tell them i don't care

while listening to them

describe the ways you've changed

here i thought you would always

stay the same

- *changed*

i envy the rains

every wet pearl

that will slide down your back

like my nails used to

when you were deep inside

of me

in my pussy

in my asshole

in my mouth

when you were . . .

- *deep inside*

we shed tears over those who

leave us

when we should express joy

over those who have stayed

- *loyal*

sometimes it feels like

we are slow dancing

in a burning living room

i spent nights in my room atop this bed devastated by loss

i tried to cry you back

but the tears no longer flow

and you still have not returned

i pinch the lids of my eyes till they bleed

thinking i am living a dream

and if i hurt myself enough

i will wake up in your arms again

i will wake from this nightmare

- *wake*

it's what we could've built

had you stayed

not the collapsed mess we left behind

that hits me like

a wrecking ball

why do you

cut yourself

with the blade

my body cries

because the wounds i slice into my body

heal much quicker than

the words they have carved into my mind

I tell her

- *self-harm*

all those wishes wasted

on shooting stars

like empty cups

on the counters of dingy bars

we fool ourselves into believing

we can find a genie in a liquor bottle

or streaking across the sky

because our lives lack that magic

we hope to find before the day we die

- alcoholic

rupi! you must sit like a woman!

my father used to say

how should a woman should sit?

i asked

like your brother does!

he yelled

- *transgender*

the relation between daughter and father is like that

between wind and grass

the grass must bend

when the wind blows across it

- *i love you father*

tell them my blood

ran warm

until you chilled me to the bone

the irony of loneliness

is talking to yourself

when no one is around to hear you

at anytime

answering yourself

since we came out of our mother's belly

we have been born to die

crying and full of blood

soon we will return to that darkness

we inch forward to it like

we were pushed towards the light

- *full circle*

first

you must be the worm before

you could be

the butterfly

- *maturation comes with time*

go fuck yourself

he said

it was the last time i took a man's words seriously

and it felt better cause i know my body better than he ever did

- *self-love*

how can you try to imitate light

with so much

darkness inside you

look at what they've done

the moon cried to the earth

they've scarred my entire body

- craters from domestic abuse

my mother sacrificed herself for me

her dreams

for mine

and one day

i will sacrifice myself

and my dreams

for you

- *sacrifice yourself*

on the last day of hate

you punched me across the face

with the word

cunt

i feel anxious

cause falling in love with you

means falling out of love with him

i want to keep you both

one can take the front

and the other can have the back

- *they call it a spit-roast*

i will welcome

a lover

who will make the same

or as more as i do

because anything less

is not my equal

so match my hustle

cause i will not sleep with a loser

some guy making sandwiches at subway

or cleaning floors at a school or theater

or pouring my coffee at a bagel store

go back to school and get a degree

you loser

get a real job

a career job

- *no scrubs*

do not feel quilty for telling the truth

- honesty is rare like the unicorn

a

man

who sobs

*- a beta who likely wears flannel shirts white capri pants
and sandals to brunch*

this evening

i told the mexican deliveryman

what i'd do to you

and he said

cuatro pesos loca puta

- he smiled at me

when your body

is in my body

you begin

where i end

there is no two

there is only one

you

and

me

are one person

- *reverse cowgirl sex*

i am

made of mostly water and blood and muscles and bones

of course i will cry

i will bleed

i will strain and tear

and

i will break if you push me too far

it was as though

someone had shoved a

wet cucumber up my ass

- *first time anal*

the moon envies

your

shine

- *envy*

upon my entry

as the doctor delivered me

my mother said

christ how we will afford this one now

if we leave right now before signing anything

does that mean it belongs to you?

- proud momma

i want to wake up in a room

where love is plastered to the walls

like my back as he becomes one with me

my legs over his shoulders

my nails down his back

his testicles slapping off

of my tight asshole

- fuck me on a sunday morning before brunch

how little

or how much

clothing she has on her brown body

has nothing to do with the fact she

feels free

covered or

uncovered

- *liberated*

sharing the same artery

the same blood

the same battered heart

does not make us sisters

sharing the same body that has

endured the same hardships

the same prejudices

the same abuses

the same torment

this

and only this

is why i say we are all

sisters

cause we share the same scars

the same body

- *the same*

i foolishly thought

'tween me and you

our love would stand the test of time

and never ever fade

but we are not making love no more

we're not even trying to change

tell me

how did it all slip away

can we ever have what we had yesterday?

you'll never fly

my mother said

if you are afraid of heights

- take a leap off of the ledge with your arms out

here's to the pawns

to the bishops

to the knights

the kings and queens

for without them

the pieces would not move themselves into

battles

and there would be

no wars to die over

- *chess / life / politics*

as a child

my mother used to kiss my heels

when i lost my balance

saying to me tenderly

your roots are weak

if your foundations are not built around

love and proper nourishment

- photosynthekiss

when i am pregnant with my daughter

i will speak to her like

she has already changed the universe

she will shoot out of me like a comet

leaving a trail of knowledge behind

that will have others looking up to her

if the road to

changing the world

was never-ending

our bodies would need more gas

- *fill me up*

i see no changes

all i see is racist faces

misplaced hate is a disgrace to races

we under

i often wonder what it takes to make this

a better place lets erase the wasted

take the evils out the people and

they will start acting right

cause both black and brown is

smoking crack tonight

and only time we care is when we

kill one another

it takes skill to be real

it is time we heal each other

it is not a secret to conceal the fact

the prisons are packed and

they are filled with browns and blacks

but some things will never change

trying to show them other ways

- we need to change

they say

she is lucky

that rupi is a star

but i cry cry cry in my lonely heart thinking

if there's nothing missing in my life

then why do i cry every night?

- *unlucky*

i said one winter morning

fall gently

cover me with white icy kisses

on my tongue you taste like heaven

on my body you feel

like his cold embrace

like him you

melt into my flesh

i can wash you off of my body

but his unwanted touches can

never be washed off

- stained

we are raised from timidity

my mother said

we dare be brave

until we suddenly see

love costs all that we are

and will ever be

yet it is only love

that can ever set us free

- my mother's words

we all are starving

yet have no idea

until we have reached the end of the table that

we left the banquet behind us

rushing through life filling our pockets

dying just as fast with empty souls

- *broke from within*

he was the first male you

ever loved

in his arms he held you

protected you from the world

you called him daddy

now you are sleeping in the arms of another man

you call him daddy too

but only when he pulls your hair back and

fucks you hard doggystyle with a thumb up your asshole

- big daddy

why are we attracted to toxic people

but insist our foods be organic?

- *contradictions*

a daughter who

begs her father for a

relationship

will beg her

abusive boyfriend for

commitment

never realizing she was better off alone

- *castles in the sky*

your mother joined the habit

and you prayed she

would come home

and after you got up

off your knees

the priest had

finished fondling his bone

a war bordering two countries

damage on both sides

collateral

there is a paradox in this

splitting them apart

keeps the politicians bank accounts

as fat as their waistlines

- war is profitable

father, you rarely call and when you do

nothing comes across on your end

sometimes you ask what i'm doing or

where i am but only when

i've said nothing sitting on the toilet straining

to hear you and cause i'm constipated

when it all does finally come out

and you say a few words that

in your weird way is meant to convey love

i'm done taking a shit and i am done with

you

- *emancipated / constipated*

i can't tell if my father is

frightened or still in love with

my mother it all

looks the same to me

i flinch when i hear

loud noises like

thunder or gunshots

so i eat foods that will not give

me gas

one time i farted while sleeping and

scared myself awake so badly my heart

was racing out of my chest

sounded like a machine gun had gone off

what am i to you

he asks

as he slams his entire cock into

my ass

from behind

my fuck toy

i say while

reaching for my swollen clitoris

- this is called a reach around my sisters

i can't love him if

i haven't learned how

to love myself

- *masturbate*

i once told a black boy

the first boy i ever wanted

i am ready for you

i have always been ready for that

thick black cock

you will never orgasm like you will

with any other kind of cock

white ones are small

yellow ones are too thin and small

brown ones are short and stinky

try a black one my sisters

often you

leave me speechless

my tongue is tied

truth is

you make me forget what

language I speak in

but our bodies say plenty

coiled under bed sheets

- *busy tongues*

without having

touched me

you've

touched me

i heard your voice

you undressed my mind

my body soon followed

on nights

like this

i need you to

run me a bath

brush my hair

rub my feet

and use your mouth to

get me to orgasm

- rough day

i've had enough black coffee

looking at you has shown me that

it is time i tried drinking it

light and sweet

i love you

he whispered

whatever

i said

the key is to not fall for

the games men play

- *play hard to get my sisters*

it wasn't you i was blowing

—don't be foolish

it was his cock on my mind

yours was just available

why do i always

come back to you

circles in the parking lot

sitting on the porch steps

keys always in my hand

eyes staring at the lock

i always come back

to you

- *why do i*

my tongue got used to

your taste

so i can't tell the difference between

sour or sweet

it's all the same to me

build me into your life

if you wish

but what i really want is

to build a life

with you

- under construction

how can i put ink to paper if

when he left he

bled my heart dry

my macbook runs on power

i run on vibes

and right now

my cells are dying

- *he was my charger*

if i knew

splitting myself open would

hurt this much

i don't think i would

bother sewing myself up afterward

- *bleed out on the kitchen floor*

he won't be coming back

muttered my head

he will and he will bring roses and dark chocolate

sobbed my heart

- wish fulfillment

i have lost parts of you like

hair from my scalp in the shower drain

like bits of sanity

i no longer have

i have tried to glue those hairs back

on my head

but they

much like you

no longer belong to me

it all belongs to the darkness

you left and

ask if i can come with you

while you have someone else

in your passenger seat

i cannot be the third wheel

in a car built for two

- *when you try to keep me around as a friend with benefits*

when they tell you they love you

look at their actions

don't listen to the words of men

they have been trained to speak lies

to build castles in the skies

promising us jobs and jewelry

but look at your wrists

those are fake diamonds he gave you

the apartment you stand in

it isn't even a penthouse suite

last night you ate the cheapest cut of steak

and he didn't even offer to cut it for you

a glass of wine that tasted flat

you were better off with

that jewish guy who owned the jewelry store

down the block

he was older and balding but

he has a good job and comes from a good family

and now the cable is out because he

didn't have enough money this month to

pay the bill

how will you go horseback riding on the weekend

if he is already broke

so this weekend you will just have to stay in

and watch movies with him on the couch again

no no no, this has to stop

it is time you left him

he doesn't love you because if he did

you wouldn't be living in such despicable conditions

real men know how to treat queens when they see them

- you are a queen do not forget that my sister

monday

you say you are just

a friend of mine

tuesday

we played some games

wednesday

you left again

thursday

things just weren't the same

on friday

you came back with roses and baklava

i wanted to kiss you

on saturday

we saw our lovers

on sunday

we made love

now what are going to do

what are we going to do

- *seven days of games*

i can build a home

out of all the bricks

they have thrown at me

- *those that have doubted me*

i once believed

love would be

burning red like a wildfire

until you showed me

love can also be blue

like a cold dead body

and that is how i feel

i took your matches before

you could set me on fire

you did a number on me

but baby

who is counting

you held onto

your pride

like you should have

held onto me

my heart

is the proof

you

are a breaker of

promises

papa

i sang softly

while running towards him

can i have another cup of

milk and honey

i ran circles around him and my

pet goat

darka-lark

making sounds like a train i did

choo choo

choo choo

his big brown hand came down

across my face like a

block of sun baked ham

wack

i fell on the dirt path as he said

the fuck is wrong with you rupi

dumbass fucking girl

now you scared the goat

and i still have to shave its back

if love is a battlefield

why are we

fighting each other

in a war none of us

will ever win

- *i surrender*

removing the hair from

your privates is okay

if you want to

just as much as keeping

that hair below your navel

is also okay

if you want to

- *don't let society tell you what is appropriate*

you were a bird

long before he came and

put you in a cage

and after he's left

you will fly

like you did before

why do you cry

i whispered into my mother's ears

because i hurt all over

she cried

i wrap my arms around her and say

but you can heal

there is

a goddess between your legs

many men will want to bow

at your altar

don't mistake begging with prayers

what you possess is the power of

life

- *sisterhood*

seva

i practice this daily
a homeless mother with
kids at her sides sat
on a piece of cardboard
with a paper cup asking for change
i gave her enough money to
buy her kids food for the night
i had no money left for myself
and she had nothing to give me
in return for what i gave her
but her smile was enough payment

- *selfless is something more of us need to do daily*

nana said

knock you out

rupi you knock them out

or i'm going to

knock you out

- time to fight back against the patriarchy my sisters

i want to make love

to you in a gazebo

under the influence of love

they call it a placebo

it's so rich they call it

jeff bezos

- making love under the feet of god

the only drug i've ever taken

kept me high as a seagull all night

most mornings too

flowing through my veins

pumping through my heart

no needles stuck in my arms

no pills down my throat

or powders up my nose

I had to go to rehab

my mom said

go go go

but i said

oh oh oh

i was addicted to you

but we were born

to die

- *born to die*

there's many things i

want to say to you

but i know you want to live

like if you hold me without

hurting me

you'll be the first

who ever did

my love

love has nothing to do with

what you are expecting

to get

only with what you are

expecting to give

—which is everything

- *everything*

whatever our souls

are made of

his and mine are

the same

- *soulmates*

love is madness

but there is always

reason in madness

lots of people want to ride with me

in the limo

i want the few that will take

the bus with me

when the limo has broken down

love is sent from heaven

to

worry the hell out of you and me

i've always wanted to be

an irresistible desire

that is

irresistibly desired

my whole life

i have said sorry for the things

i know i should have done

many things i could have said

instead i stayed silent

sometimes i wish i had said those words

seems i'm always a little too late

- too late

i met some ghosts

on my travels

through america's midwest

in costumes but

halloween was months away

- *early trick or treaters*

use your hands

mother said tenderly

to life those that cannot

pick themselves up

like a crab on its back

you won't allow me

to help you find your way

you will die here if you don't let me

but still you use your claws to

fight me off

i must go then

your shell has made you

—hardheaded

if i could be anything

in this universe

i want to be his sun

lighting his way

through the dark

providing him with warmth

a way out

- a wish upon a star

there is no reason

to look back

when you have so much

to look forward to

- *look ahead*

let's

fckn'

get

it

- rally cry for sisterhood

it hurts to speak

in front of so many people

it hurts to speak

in front of no one

then i wake up

and find myself sipping coffee

at the counter of starbucks

looking past a glass window stained

with bird shit and spit

here i sit daydreaming of the day

you will walk through that door

and ask me

if we could share a pumpkin spice latte

if we could post a selfie with the drink

smiling like we are the first to buy one

crying because i know we will never

have another upload together

- i no longer buy pumpkin spice anything because of you

if i do what she will not do

will you choose me

if i give you that which

she will not

will it make your decision

easier

command me

why are you ashamed of me

my body sobs

cause you are the reason they laugh at us

i reply

it means i am ready

to bring life

into the world

it means

i am a woman

- *menstruation / period*

i want to be like

khaleesi

but i do not want her dragons

i have my protector

my pet goat

darka-lark

when it's winter

i wish for summer

when it's rainy

i wish for clear skies

when you were here

i wanted you gone

- *hormones*

i've learned people will forget

what you've said

forget what you've done

but they won't forget how

you made them feel

there is no greater pain than

bearing an untold story

inside you

we praise the beauty of

the butterfly

but look past the changes it

has gone through to

show the world how true beauty

radiates from the inside out

- inside out / lesson learned

even ugly ducklings turn into

beautiful swans

you may not be able to control

what happens to you in life

but you can control how life

happens to you

- perspective

never make someone a priority

when all you are to them

is a convenient option

it is possible for

a plain yellow pumpkin to

become a golden carriage

an ugly duckling to become a

lovely swan someday

- believe in yourself

i've always been in love with you

i cried

he shrugged uncaringly

i guess you've always known it's true

you took my love for granted

why oh why

he shook his head and his mask fell off

this show is over say goodbye

- and the oscar goes to

my mother always told me

smile and put on a happy face

all the world loves a clown

so i put on my makeup and

go on stage to perform

they laugh they smile

it comes so easy

when i wash this mask off after

the show has ended and i have

left the circus

the real joke begins

on me

there is nothing funny here

why are you laughing at me

stop talking about me

as a kid we love the heroes

as adults we understand the villians

- joker / mental health awareness

they want to

silence me

- *silence of the kaur*

i used to think of my life as

a tragedy

now i realize it is a

comedy

- *they call this a paradox my lovelies*

i wish

i could quit you

but we are one and

the same

how can you be sure things

are better

if you can't be sure your heart

is still here with me

caged like a sparrow

pecking into my bones to feed on

my marrow

we were destined to always be together

don't you remember being struck with

cupid's arrow

- *cupid has awful aim*

you make me feel like a

toilet bowl

taking your shit

- *a metaphor*

who are we to tell

two similar batteries that they

can't be together

after all

it takes two like batteries to

brighten up our paths

- *pro lgbtq*

i want to give

eskimo kisses to

lady gaga

- *caught in a bad romance*

we will always be

young and beautiful

one surgery away from

holding onto a part of us

that time has come to take

hair dye coloring in grey roots

i am too vain to allow time to

take anymore of my youth

my few reminders that

i was once a woman

that was often called

young and beautiful

i've had anal

she said shyly

but i don't know what a

dirty sanchez is

- explore your sexuality

if you nail my feet

to the ground with that

nail of a tongue

your mouth like a hammer

how will i

ever stand up for myself

but that's the point of your

verbal abuse

to keep me floored like a carpet

you act like my biggest fan

following me around like

paparazzi

photographing my every movement

but i'm nothing special

as a matter of fact sometimes i

feel like

a piece of shit

- just being honest

what i can't stand is women

tearing other women down

when will we realize

friendly fire is anything but

friendly

i'm sorry

but i've given others so much

that i have nothing left

inside me to give to you

- *charity*

the last thing we should do

during a virus outbreak

is to spread fear and

lies about our fellow humans

what we should be doing is coming together

and embracing each other so that

we could find a cure through love and

compassion

- *love can cure what the medications only manage*

how does it feel

to know your daughter

sleeps with men that

abuse her like you did

that tell her

she is worth nothing

that beat on her like

a punching bag when drunk

that take her whenever they want

even if she refuses to be taken

still they take

they take until she has been left

with nothing

so tell me

how does it feel

- *father*

here we are

at the most crucial time in human history

floating aimlessly

among this global mess others

before us created

one our elders refused to acknowledge

that it is their trash at our feet

and they scream at us

you clean that up kid

my dearest friend greta said it best

how dare you

- we deserve a safe future / a future without plastic bags

CPSIA information can be obtained
at www.ICGtesting.com
Printed in the USA
LVHW050951290122
709476LV00014B/2089